Clever Trevor

by Sarah Albee
illustrated by Paige Billin-Frye

The Kane Press
New

Acknowledgements: Our thanks to Marc Feldman, PhD (Physics, UC Berkeley), Professor, University of Rochester, for helping us make this book as accurate as possible.

Library of Congress Cataloging-in-Publication Data

Albee, Sarah.
  Clever Trevor / by Sarah Albee ; illustrated by Paige Billin-Frye.
     p. cm. — (Science solves it!)
Summary: In an attempt to reclaim the playground, Trevor figures out how to use an uneven seesaw to teach Buzz and his bully buddies a lesson.
  ISBN: 978-1-57565-123-1 (alk. paper)
  [1. Levers—Fiction. 2. Bullies—Fiction. 3. Seesaw—Fiction.] I. Billin-Frye, Paige, ill.
II. Title. III. Series.
  PZ7.A3174 Cl 2003
  [E]—dc21
                                                                    2002010661

10 9 8 7 6 5

First published in the United States of America in 2003 by Kane Press, Inc.
Printed at Worzalla Publishing, Stevens Point, WI, U.S.A., May 2012.

Science Solves It! is a registered trademark of Kane Press, Inc.

Book Design/Art Direction: Edward Miller

Visit us online at **www.kanepress.com**

 Like us on Facebook
facebook.com/kanepress

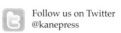 Follow us on Twitter
@kanepress

"Don't look now. Here they come," said Kyle under his breath.

Of course, Amanda and I *did* look. Sure enough, the three bullies were heading straight toward us.

"They're going to take over the playground again," Amanda said nervously.

Our playground was nothing fancy. The slide was a little wobbly. The seesaw was uneven. And the hoops had no nets. But ever since we were little, my friends and I had loved hanging out there—that is, until the bullies started showing up.

"Pretend we don't see them," said Kyle.

Amanda took a shot. It clanged off the rim. We watched the ball bounce right up to the biggest bully.

He stooped down and picked it up with one hand. I couldn't help noticing that his hand was the size of my baseball glove.

"Uh, you guys want to play a game of three on three?" I asked.

"Hear that, Buzz? Hear that, Nicki?" snorted Rocky. "They want to play three on three."

Nicki snickered, then looked at Buzz.

"That's pretty funny," said Buzz. But he didn't laugh. "Why don't you little squirts run along and play?"

I wanted to say something really clever back, but all that came out was, "Oh, yeah?"

Buzz took a step closer. "Yeah. *Scram.*"
We scrammed.

Amanda and Kyle bounced up and down on the seesaw. "This stinks," muttered Kyle. "Every day they kick us off our court. Now they're even using our *ball.*"

"Yeah," said Amanda. "We end up on the seesaw like a bunch of babies. I'm tired of sitting here, watching them play."

"You could switch places with Kyle,"
I joked. "That way you wouldn't have to watch."

"I can't," sighed Amanda.

"Why not?" I asked.

Amanda shrugged. "This old seesaw doesn't work when we switch places. Kyle gets stuck on the bottom and I get stuck on the top."

I stared at the seesaw. Why does that happen? Kyle is a lot bigger than Amanda. Could that have something to do with it?

"Hey, Earth to Trevor," said Amanda.
"It's getting late. We'd better go."

That night after supper, I built a model seesaw in the basement. I made it uneven, just like the one on the playground.

I took a bag of cat food and put it on the short end of the board. I pushed down on the long end with my foot. It was easy to lift.

Next I put the cat food on the *long* end of the board and pushed down on the *short* end. *Oof!* I could hardly budge it. My socks slipped out from under me, and I wiped out.

Right that second my sister Beth walked in. "Very graceful," she giggled. Then she saw my model. "What's with the lever, Trevor?"

"The what?" I asked.

Beth rolled her eyes. "That's a **lever,**" she said. "Levers are lifting machines. We studied them in science."

She pointed out the different parts.

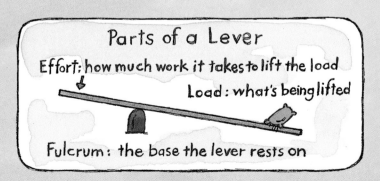

Parts of a Lever

Effort: how much work it takes to lift the load

Load: what's being lifted

Fulcrum: the base the lever rests on

Then she said, "You know, it would be easier to lift the bag of cat food if you put it on the short end."

"Yeah, I noticed that," I said.

Aha! Suddenly everything started to make sense. Now I understood why Kyle had to sit on the short end of the seesaw!

That's when it hit me. Maybe this lever stuff could help me get rid of the bullies.

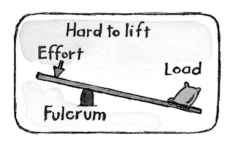

Hard to lift
Effort
Load
Fulcrum

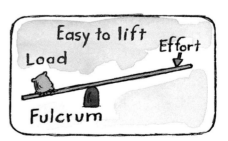

Easy to lift
Load
Effort
Fulcrum

"Suppose I want to make something hard to lift," I said to Beth. "I should put it *far* from the fulcrum. Right?"

"Right. I see genius runs in the family," said Beth. "But why would you want to make something hard to lift?"

I just smiled.

The next day, I got to the playground after Amanda and Kyle. The bullies were already on the basketball court. I walked straight toward them.

"Uh, Trev?" said Kyle. "Are you nuts?"

"Hey, Buzz," I called. "Want to have a contest?"

Buzz was so surprised, he dribbled the ball off his own foot.

"I bet I can prove I'm stronger than you,"
I said. "If I can, we get our playground back."
Buzz smirked. "Okay, squirt. But if you
lose, you've got to find another playground.
No more hanging out here—*ever*. Got it?"
Gulp. "Got it," I said.

Kyle's and Amanda's mouths hung open. They watched the bullies follow me over to the seesaw.

"Have a seat on the lev—I mean, on the seesaw," I said. I patted the short end.

Buzz glared at me, but he sat down.

I went over to the long end. I pushed down hard with one hand. Buzz rose up in the air.

"Big deal," he said.

I let Buzz back down. Then I climbed onto my end of the seesaw.

"Now you lift me," I said.

Buzz pushed down on the short end of the seesaw with one hand. A puzzled look crossed his face. He pushed down with two hands. He could barely lift me.

"What's the matter, Buzz?" Nicki asked him.

"Yeah," said Rocky. "What's the matter?"

"This guy's super-heavy!" Buzz said angrily. "He must have rocks in his pockets!"

I hopped off the seesaw and walked over to Buzz. I pulled my pockets inside out so he could see they were empty.

"It looks like I *am* stronger than you," I
said. "Now we get our playground back—
and our ball."

"Wow," whispered Amanda.

"Amazing!" said Kyle.

Everyone was staring at me—everyone except Buzz. He looked like he was about to blow steam out his ears.

He kicked the seesaw hard. "Ow!" he howled. Then he started limping off the playground.

"Let's go!" he snarled at the others.

The next day, Kyle, Amanda, and I were shooting baskets. Suddenly Kyle said, "They're back!"

Sure enough, Buzz, Nicki, and Rocky were heading our way.

Buzz stopped right in front of me. "I'm on to you," he said. "It took me a while, but I figured out your little lever trick."

As soon as Buzz said that, I remembered something. *Buzz was in my sister's grade!* That meant he knew all about levers.

I was toast!

But all of a sudden, Buzz grinned. Then he slapped me on the back so hard I started to cough.

"You know something?" he said. "For a little squirt, you're pretty clever, Trevor."

"Thanks," I said. Maybe Buzz isn't so bad after all, I thought to myself.

"How about a game of three on three?" asked Buzz.

I looked at Kyle and Amanda. They both nodded quickly.

"You're on," I said.

These days we all meet at the playground. One time Buzz even brought his dad to fix the seesaw. He said that was to make sure I didn't play any more lever tricks.

And guess what? Buzz even stopped calling me squirt.

I can make a model!

THINK LIKE A SCIENTIST

Trevor thinks like a scientist—and so can you! Scientists make models. They use models to find out how something works. They also use models to help explain their ideas.

Look Back
On page 10, what did Trevor notice about Kyle and Amanda? On page 12, what did he observe about the seesaw? Look at pages 12–15. How did Trevor's observations help him make a model of the seesaw? What materials did he use? What did he discover?

Try This!
Make your own model of Trevor's model!
You will need:

- a wooden ruler
- a marker
- a weight, such as a can of tuna

Rest the ruler on the marker.

First put the weight on the short end of the ruler. Raise the weight by pushing down on the ruler's long end with your index finger.

Now put the weight on the long end of the ruler. Push down on the short end.

Did you get the same results that Trevor did?